This book belongs to:

_____

STICKS GO WALKING

by Georgianna Pfost

Illustrated by George Franco and Mara Erika Licardo

~ Purple Cotton Candy Arts ~

To C's Sticks from St. P's
and their descendants at the Micke Grove Zoo

Text copyright © 2022 Georgianna Pfost

Illustration copyright © 2022 George Franco and Mara Erika Licardo

First published in 2022 by Purple Cotton Candy Arts
Sacramento, California
www.purplecottoncandyarts.com

Printed in the United States of America

Library of Congress Control Number: 2022903811

ISBN: 978-1-7374406-6-6

"Beautiful!" Sue sighed as she, Stu, and their eight companions stretched out in their summer home.

"And the blackberry leaves were delicious!" replied Stu.

A boy's fingers pulled back the terrarium's screened lid and removed the leftovers before adding fresh leaves and a spray of water.

"Ready to play?" called Lisa, dribbling a basketball across the kitchen toward her brother. "Oh, are those the bugs you brought home from school for the summer?"

"In a minute, and yea, they're Walking Sticks," Tony responded as he grabbed the dry stems and ran across the backyard to toss them onto the compost pile.

In his hurry, he didn't notice that two of the twigs were actually Sue and Stu.

"Oops!" exclaimed Sue. "I don't think we're supposed to be out here."

"No, and we'd better try to get back before dark," agreed Stu.

As they looked around at the grass clippings and potato peelings, a small head popped up.

"Who are you?" asked Sue, stepping closer as a long, legless creature emerged.

"Me? I'm an Earthworm. Who are you?"

"We're Stick Bugs," Sue replied.

"Does that mean you eat sticks?" asked Earthworm. "I sort of eat earth while I tunnel through it."

"No, we just look like sticks," stated Stu. "We eat leaves, but we need to get back to the kitchen."
"It's across the yard," pointed Earthworm with its tail.

Sue and Stu thanked Earthworm and started climbing out when a flying creature about a third their size landed on the bin's edge.

"Who are you?" it inquired, eyes wide.

"We're Stick Bugs," Stu replied. "Who are you?"
"I'm a Soldier Fly, but I don't fight. I lay my eggs in the compost so my children can eat. Is that why you're here?"

"We got dropped here by mistake," explained Sue. "We live in a terrarium indoors and eat fresh leaves."

"Then you'll want to head to the garden across the walkway," advised Fly as it flew into the bin. "But it's nice to meet you!"

Sue and Stu climbed over the edge and down the outside of the bin.

"Flying must save time," murmured Stu.

"But we're Walking Sticks," noted Sue.

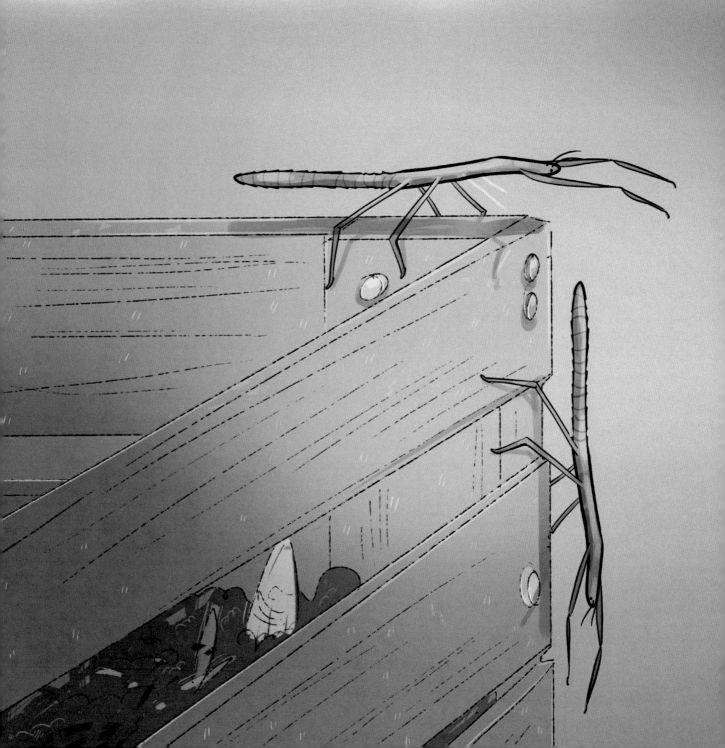

As they reached the ground, a small brown creature about Fly's size hopped out from under a board. "Oh!" it declared. "I thought you were twigs!"

"We're Stick Bugs," said Sue. "Who are you?"
"I'm a Cave Cricket!" it chirped. "But there aren't any caves here, just holes under rocks and boards."

"We're heading back to the kitchen," Stu added, "but looking for blackberry leaves to snack on."

"Berries are near the fence," said Cricket, pointing with an antenna.

"Thanks!" the Sticks chorused as Cricket hopped off.

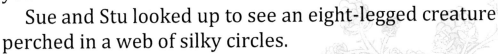

Sue and Stu soon found the thorny vines. A faint "who are you?" sounded from above.

Sue and Stu looked up to see an eight-legged creature perched in a web of silky circles.

"Hello!" Stu replied. "We're Walking Sticks, looking for a leaf snack. And you are?"

"I wouldn't have noticed you except you were walking," chuckled the creature. "I'm a Garden Spider because I live in one."

"Names aren't always too precise," declared a voice below.

The trio looked down to see a slender, shiny creature with pinchers at the rear.

"Meet Earwig, also known as Pincher Bug," announced Spider.

"Do you listen or pinch a lot?" Stu asked.

"No," answered Earwig "but I do eat leaves."

"Let's grab a quick bite," said Sue, "and then find some water."

They climbed under a leaf and began munching. A low buzzing made them look up to see a round, fuzzy creature landing on a flower.

"You must be the Stick Bugs!" it buzzed. "I saw you moving into the kitchen yesterday."

"Yes, that's us," said Stu. "And you are?"

"I'm a Carpenter Bee," it replied, "but I don't nail or saw. I nest in the old fence post."

"We're looking for the kitchen," noted Sue.
"It's past the vegetable garden," Bee explained.
"Thanks!" Stu called as Bee buzzed that way.

The two Sticks climbed down and started through the garden when a white-winged creature silently landed on a plant beside them.

"Who are you?" it asked.

"We're Stick Bugs," explained Sue patiently, "because we look like sticks."

"Well, I'm a Cabbage Moth," it twittered, "but I don't look like cabbage. I lay my eggs there so my caterpillars can eat the leaves."

"We eat leaves, too," said Sue, "but now we're looking for water."

"There's a bowl on the porch," said Moth.

"Thanks!" called Sue and Stu, and they soon came across a puddle of water by a shallow dish.

As they sipped, a metallic-looking bug about their size hovered to the edge of the bowl on its four wings.

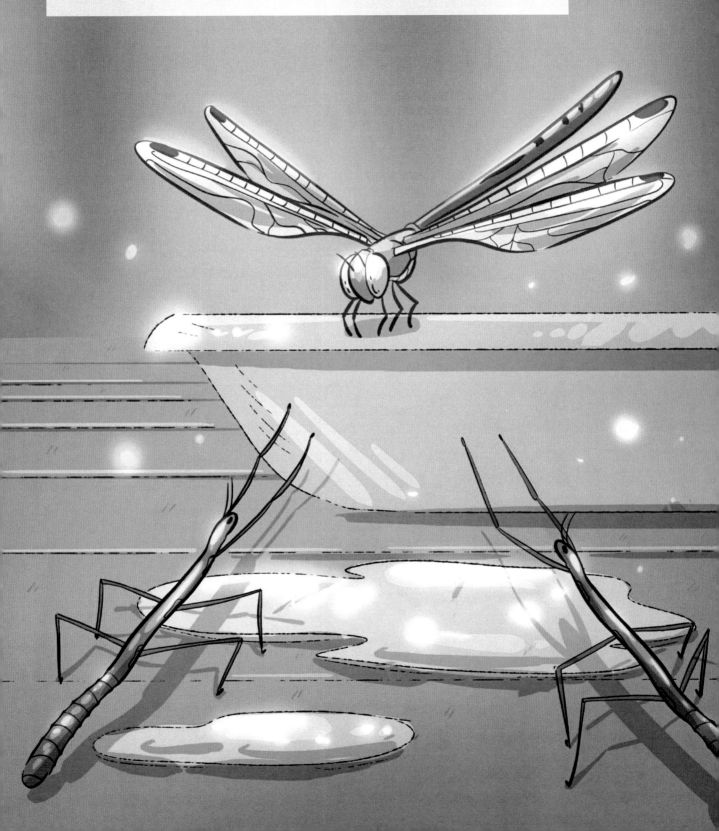

"Who are you?" gasped Sue.
"I'm Dragon Fly," it replied. "And you?"

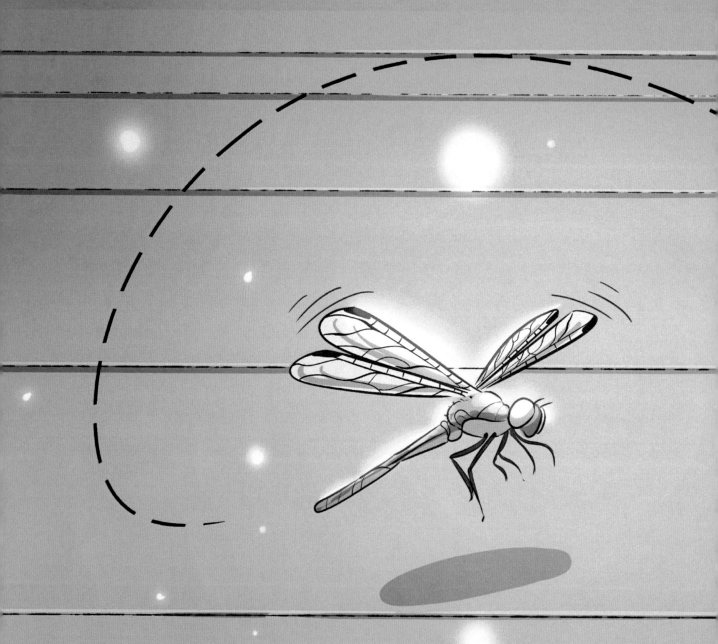

"We're Stick Bugs," said Sue, "if you couldn't tell. You don't look like a dragon!"

"No, I think the smaller bugs named me that," it mused. You do look like sticks, though," it added as it flew on.

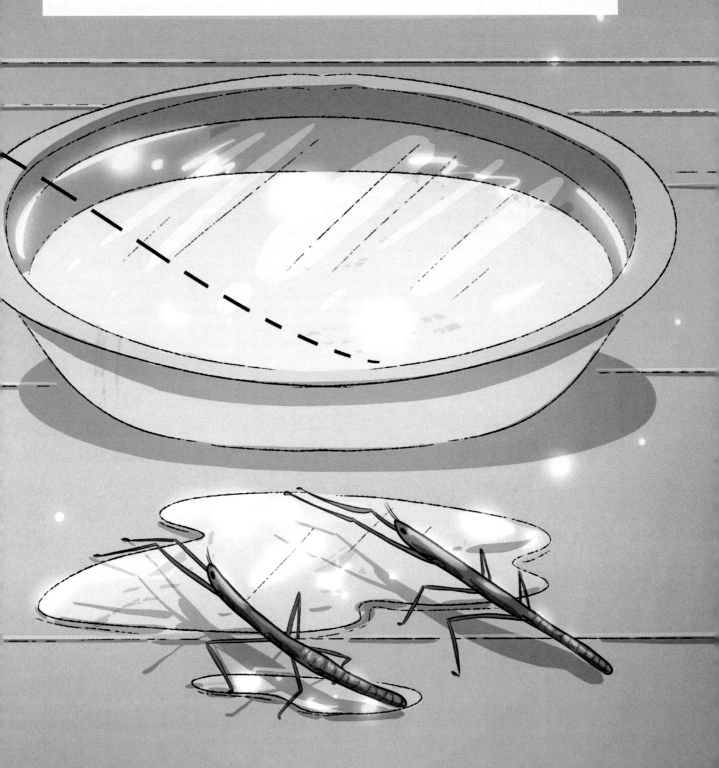

Just then a long, furry creature appeared, sniffing the ground as it neared the bowl.

"One of Tony's dogs!" Sue murmured and froze in place.

"Taffy, what have you found now?" Tony called as he rushed after the dachshund.

"Oh, good! The missing Stick Bugs!" he exclaimed, kneeling to scoop them onto his arm.

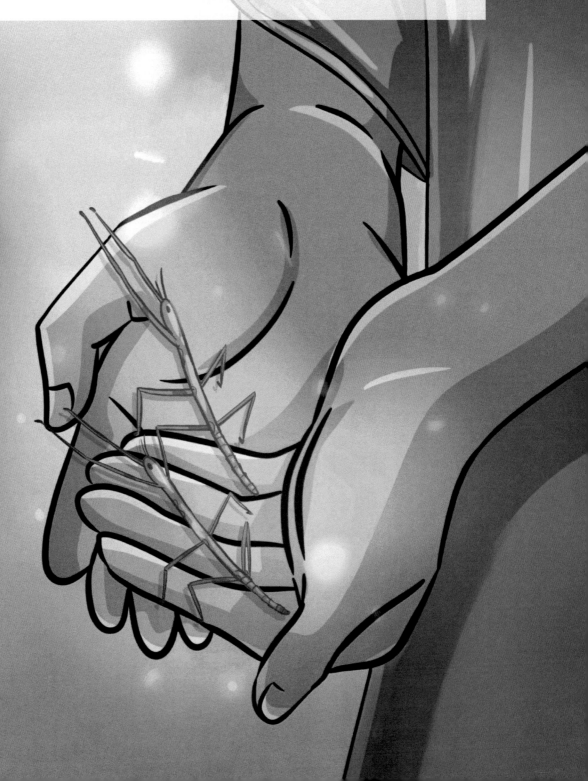

"I found them!" he called to Lisa as he entered the kitchen. "I wondered why I only saw eight when we got back from the game. I must have dropped these two in the compost with the dry stems."

"Well, it's good they are *Walking* Sticks," laughed Lisa as Tony set the bugs in the terrarium. "They must have had quite an adventure!"

"We sure did!" whispered Stu to the other Sticks gathered around.

And late that night, when the people were asleep, Sue and Stu told their tale of how Sticks go walking.

A NOTE TO READERS

This book is a fictionalized account of the tiny creatures I've found in my backyard and the Sticks from my stepson's school, which vacationed in our kitchen. I hope it gives a glimpse of some of the often overlooked but interesting "bugs" you may find in your own yard or nearby park and how each fills a niche in our local and global ecosystems.

The Annam Walking Sticks in this story are just one of about 3,000 species of Stick insects that use their plant-like appearance for camouflage. The neighbors they meet represent a few of the other million known insect species, 80,000 spider species, and 1,800 earthworm species on our planet.

To learn more about these creatures:

- Read about Walking Sticks and other insects, spiders, and earthworms.

- Start a list of "bugs" you've spotted (from *A*nts to *Z*orapterans).

- Draw pictures or take photos of them.

- Visit a school, zoo, or nature center with a live insect exhibit.

- Learn about "integrated pest management" and other ways to maintain a natural balance of plants and animals in your garden without using dangerous chemicals.

- Start a compost pile and watch for earthworms.

- Plant flowers to help feed pollinators like bees and moths.

Made in the USA
Columbia, SC
23 November 2022

71042643R00022